H.

CHILLERS

Wilf and
the Black Hole

HIAWYN ORAM

Illustrated by
DEE SHULMAN

PUFFIN BOOKS

CHILLERS

The Blob Tessa Potter and Peter Cottrill
Clive and the Missing Finger Sarah Garland
The Day Matt Sold Great-grandma Eleanor Allen and Jane Cope
The Dinner Lady Tessa Potter and Karen Donelly
Ghost from the Sea Eleanor Allen and Leanne Franson
Hide and Shriek! Paul Dowling
Jimmy Woods and the Big Bad Wolf Mick Gowar and Barry Wilkinson
Madam Sizzers Sarah Garland
The Real Porky Philips Mark Haddon
Sarah Scarer Sally Christie and Claudio Muñoz
Spooked Philip Wooderson and Jane Cope
Wilf and the Black Hole Hiawyn Oram and Dee Shulman

PUFFIN BOOKS

Published by the Penguin Group
Penguin Books Ltd, 27 Wrights Lane, London W8 5TZ, England
Penguin Books USA Inc., 375 Hudson Street, New York, New York 10014, USA
Penguin Books Australia Ltd, Ringwood, Victoria, Australia
Penguin Books Canada Ltd, 10 Alcorn Avenue, Toronto, Ontario, Canada M4V 3B2
Penguin Books (NZ) Ltd, 182–190 Wairau Road, Auckland 10, New Zealand

Penguin Books Ltd, Registered Offices: Harmondsworth, Middlesex, England

First published by A&C Black (Publishers) Ltd 1994
Published in Puffin Books 1996
1 3 5 7 9 10 8 6 4 2

Filmset in Meridien

Made and printed in England by William Clowes Ltd, Beccles and London

Chapter One

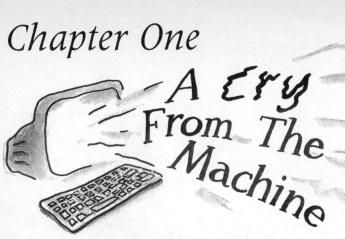

A Cry From The Machine

We'd been begging for a games machine for ages and now, at last, we had one.

Our dad said it was a kind of Bravery Award. For moving towns and changing schools and losing all our old friends.

Probably he'd have given us two if he'd known we also had to risk having our shins kicked in every day by our new school's school bully: Marigold Toecaps Garotter Barnes.

Still, he didn't know and we didn't tell and anyway we were quite happy because with the machine came an incredible game.

And in a few days, playing as often as we could, which sadly wasn't every minute, we were both on Level Five and going for Six.

ZARCO
THE DRAGON
SLAYER

AND THE UNHOLY
DOGS OF GRAIL

Only then came the night of the cry and skill-levels became the last thing on our minds, I can tell you.

Our parents were out. The babysitter was our neighbour's Spanish cousin who could only say "hello", "goodbye", and "bedtime boys" in English.

And to top it all there was this storm.

There'd be a roll of thunder. And then *nothing*. A sizzle of lightning and dead quiet. A burst of hushed, heavy raindrops and then zero. Just a long electric stillness till the next low growl.

"Come on," I said, to take our minds off the weirdness, "let's pretend the Dogs are that Marigold Toecaps."

Yeah, OK! said Eric, my brother.

And then, there it was. Right then.

One of the Unholy Dogs we were pretending was Toecaps, turned and *looked at us.*

Eric breathed.

I lied.

But I had seen it and I saw and heard what happened next.

The Unholy Dog looked at us again.

And from out of its mouth came a word. A blobby, glinky, audioklunky, *blood-freezing* word. A word you couldn't ignore if your heart was wood, since it was less of a word and more of a cry.

That cry was

Chapter Two

Eric grabbed the controls, his eyes like white saucers.

he shouted.

I shouted back.

The game took the Unholy Dog round the palace and right into Zarco's path.

Normally we'd have had Zarco missile it but Eric let them collide so the game was over and the New Game Graphics filled the screen.

And the Unholy Dog was there even though it shouldn't have been till Level Two.

Its mouth came up close against the screen. B..A..R.T it glinked.

My heart went into double-time as my name is Bart, short for Bartholomew.

"It's begging you," Eric breathed.

"Ereek," said the Dog.

"And it's begging me," said Eric. "We've got to do something, quick."

"But what?" I was yelling. "It may be after US!"

"Not-after-you-just-get-me-out-of-here," it glinked.

Eric threw himself on to his knees, his face right up against the screen.

"How?" His mouth was touching the screen. You could hear the electricity zizzing and flying.

"Like-that" said the Dog.

"Like what?" said Eric, almost licking the screen.

Then suddenly his body spiralled into the air and he fell down flat, though luckily not completely electrocuted.

Chapter Three

An Unholy Dog On Our Carpet And A Presence

"Eric!" I was on my knees.

The game zapped and glunked behind me.

I glanced over my shoulder to see whether the Dog was still on the screen. Though I didn't know why I bothered since I knew exactly where it was: in Eric's brain preparing to take him over so that by the time our parents got home he'd *be* the Unholy Dog.

But just as this flashed before *my* eyes, Eric opened his. His mouth was pushed open from the inside – and out walked, as cool as ice, the *graphics* of the Unholy Dog. Down his chin. On to our carpet.

Eric was the colour of Readybrek, but he didn't seem nearly as afraid as me.

"But how did we get you out?" he said.

"E-lec-tric-ity," said the Graphics. "I-beamed-out-on-your-sparks. I-am-not-Unholy-Dog-Graphics-believe-in-me."

But before we could ask what it was, Angelica the babysitter came in.

she said.

I stuck my leg in front of the Graphics and gave her a stream of stuff about most babysitters giving us another five minutes.

But by the time she'd got the message, the Dog Graphics had vanished, leaving something far more frightening in its place.

And that something, whatever it was, was filling the room with a slurpy presence as if at any moment it was going to suck us up like a vacuum cleaner.

Now we didn't need anyone telling us to get to bed. We were up the stairs and under our duvets in seconds flat.

Chapter Four

Wilf Revealed

Our rooms are on the top floor under the roof. Lying in bed we can talk, as our doors are diagonally opposite.

After a while, when nothing seemed to have followed us, Eric spoke.

Phone Mum **please**. She left the number.

I thought about the trouble I'd be in if he'd been scared and I wouldn't phone.

OK I'm going.

Taking one step at a time, I started down the stairs, though I didn't get round the first bend. This was because the Presence, that invisible, slurp-you-up, vacuumy Presence was coming *up* the first bend.

"Look out, it's coming!" I yelled, doing a flying-leap back into bed.

But then, just as I thought we were over and done with, we weren't.

There was a polite crackle, like a crackly radio, from my table and a very calm little voice said, "It's OK, boys. Nothing's going to get you now."

And when I eventually pulled my duvet down an inch, this is what I saw.

On my table, was a light.

And the light was talking.

Of course it wasn't *actually* talking as it had no mouth. But nevertheless I could understand it, everything, naturally, and no computer audioglinks either.

Thank goodness Eric had heard it too and was under my duvet in a flash.

Relax! I was as tense as a new tennis racket and with good reason. What was a Light doing in my bedroom, talking to me in my own language? And more to the point, what was that shapeless, shadowy, Black Blob Thing doing on my table behind it?

"It's right here, folded up," said the Light. "It only got out of control while I was sorting myself out from those Dog Graphics."

"But what were you doing in them in the first place?" said Eric, finding his voice from under the bedclothes.

"It's a bit of a story," said Wilf, hopping onto my duvet, a little too close for comfort.

...But if you'll let me I'll do my best to explain...

Chapter Five

An Alien Light In My Bedroom And A Black Hole

"I was coming in
with the others,"
he/she/it said.
"Millions of us,
when something
went wrong.
Normally we come
in and out of your
atmosphere without
any trouble. But this
time I got separated
by a storm and the
next thing I knew,
I was in that
dreaded machine
of yours."

"It's the best," said Eric. "We got it for going to our new school."

"Well, it was nearly the end of me," said Wilf, "and for someone like me not to exist is almost impossible."

"What exactly are you, Mister Wilf," said Eric, "an *extraterrestrial* or something?"

"I suppose so," said Wilf. "In your terms."

But Extra-Terrestrials are green and monstery!

"Some may be," said Wilf, "but *we're* all condensed light and energy. That's how we pick up on any wavelength, transmit on any wavelength and move around the galaxies."

"But what do you do it *for*?" I said. "I mean, come here all the time?"

"On this occasion to do something about the poisonous gases your grown-ups are dumping in the atmosphere by the ton every second"

"That's where the Presence comes in. It's actually a kind of small Black Hole . . ."

I felt the cold, creeping chill again.

And probably because I was so chilled, Eric got there before me.

"You mean to *gobble them up*?"

"Right," said Wilf, "and restore the balance."

You mean...

I said, jumping up and nearly crushing Wilf,

...that right here, in my bedroom on my table..

...between my dinosaur model and my jar of pens...

...there's a BLACK HOLE?

"Yes," said Wilf calmly, "but don't panic. I can control it. However, right now, I can hear your parents coming home, so we'd better make ourselves scarce."

"Will you still be here tomorrow?" said Eric.

"Sure," said Wilf, taking the Black Hole over to the window. "You saved me, boys, and our friendship is just beginning. We'll be on the roof till morning."

"Great," said Eric.

But I wasn't so sure.

On my table, where the Black Hole had been loitering, my dinosaur model was fine and so was my jar of pens.

Except for one thing.

The jar was empty.

Chapter Six

Other Things Go Missing... ...And Wilf Comes To School

When Wilf and the Black Hole slipped through the window next morning, I didn't have the heart to bring up the missing pens.

He (I'd decided to think of him as a he) was literally glowing with excitement.

Right boys...
I've decided how I'm going to repay you for saving me from death by microchip.

"I'm going to come to school with you and help you with your thinking. In no time you'll both be top of the class."

"But won't everyone notice?" I said.

"Eyes don't see what minds aren't open to," said Wilf. "The Black Hole and I are as good as invisible on this planet. And in case you don't believe it, we'll test it on your mother."

So, dressing quickly, we went downstairs.

Now, our mother has X-ray vision and eyes in the back of her head. Normally she can spot a flea a mile off.

But, amazingly, she couldn't see Wilf shining in our hair or the shadowy Black Hole sniffing around the ceiling.

Even when the Black Hole came down to investigate her toast-making and brushed her hair like cobwebs, she didn't notice a thing.

What she did notice, however, was things suddenly going missing.

Eric's jacket from the stand.

My trainers from the hall.

Both our lunch boxes.

She was soon shouting about how they couldn't have just disappeared and was there any chance of us even trying to get to school before midday.

And all the time she was shouting, I was growing more certain I knew where the missing items were. *Inside the Black Hole, no question.* And on the walk to school I said so to Wilf.

"If you're right," said Wilf, "it would only be because it's not used to so much clutter. It'll soon settle down, you'll see."

"Well, it's not coming in to school with us," I said. "A Light in the classroom is one thing, but a Black Hole, *no way*."

"All right, all right," Wilf sounded flustered for the first time. "I'll take care of it."

And as we crossed the playground, he did. He slung the Black Hole high into a plane tree.

Then he hopped into my hair and came inside to perform nothing short of a miracle.

For a start, he seemed able to be on Eric's shoulder in his classroom and my shoulder in my classroom at the same time.

From there he read our thoughts.

Then, almost at the same time, he hopped on to our teachers' shoulders, read *their* thoughts and radioed them back to us.

Suddenly there was nothing we didn't know and nothing we couldn't do.

Well, if my teacher was pleased, I was ecstatic.

For the first time in my life, school work was a doddle. I felt about ten foot tall. Best of all, everyone started treating me as if I was ten foot tall.

said Stewart and Kameel in first break. (Did I want to play football with them? Is the Earth round and the Sun hot?)

"Thanks," I thought-through to Wilf as I dribbled round showing off my skills. "Thanks a squillion."

But for once, Wilf wasn't picking up on me. Probably because he was picking up on something at the far side of the playground.

The side where no one dared breathe because Marigold Toecaps Garotter and Gang were in it, terrorising Julian Harper.

And then, just as I was going for goal, he began telepathizing me. *"Get inside,"* came the wild vibrations.

Toecaps Garotter is advancing on you!

Chapter Seven

Wilf Won't Give In

Well, the next thing I knew, I wasn't scoring a brilliant goal. I was having my shins kicked in and being called an egghead-spod by you-know-who.

And what's more...

she announced between kicks

Great. Really great. Especially as I'd only
been an egghead-spod for half a morning
and I didn't really get pocket money.

Especially as now no one would talk to
me in case they got the barbecue
treatment by association.

Suddenly, I was the loneliest kid in the
school except that Richard Thomas still
lent me his felt-tips. And of course, I still
had Wilf hopping with shock-horror-
support on my shoulder.

"You have to do something!" he hopped as we went back into class after break. "Tell your teacher."

"Forget it," I thought-through. "No one tells on school bullies."

"Why? So grown-ups can ignore this too?" By now he was flickering so much I felt someone *had* to notice. So I made up an excuse and dashed for the cloakrooms to explain in peace.

"But here," I went on, "as soon as you tell on a bully, word gets out. The next thing you know *you're* dead meat, not the bully. It's best just to shut up and suffer."

"Not when I'm around," said Wilf, as darkly as a light could.

And don't think I'll let this drop because I won't!

And, as we walked to Swimming he started all over again. "Why, if that nasty, dangerous, bovver-booted, poxy Marigold isn't stopped *who knows how many she could destroy . . .*"

"Mmmm," I said vaguely. All I could think about was whether taking money from my mother's purse to pay Toecaps would still be called stealing.

"Then we're agreed," said Wilf. "The Poisonous One has to be dealt with."

"Maybe," I said. "Though I don't see how."

"By you standing up to her," Wilf thought-through.

By this time we were changed and wading through the showers.

Forget it!

I replied.

"And by beaming," said Wilf. "I will be in your hair every minute of lunch-break and when you think *beam* you'll be able to beam."

"*What, Toecaps Garotter?*" I burst out to some very funny looks from the others.

"Not so loud," said Wilf, "but yes, Toecaps Garotter."

"OK, OK," I said, letting everyone else go ahead and dive into the pool. "But where would I beam her to?"

"Anywhere you like," said Wilf.

"Even Mars or Australia?"

Even the dustbin!

"Then roll on
lunch-break!"
I breathed.
And to celebrate
what was looking like
escape from a Toecaps
reign of terror,
I did a massive
running bomb into
the deep end.

What did I care that I was whistled out
and sent back to the changing rooms in
disgrace?

Chapter Eight

Toecaps Is Beamed

And, finally, *finally* lunch-break that day did creep round.

And just as Wilf and I had been planning, I walked out of the dinner hall into the arms of Toecaps and Gang.

Oi boys-

-LOOK who's here.

Have you ever seen **shoes** like his?

Well, this was so below the belt, that I nearly lost my cool.

But I didn't. Instead I said, "What! You wanna get me for wearing sandals because my trainers were eaten by a Black Hole?"

Not comprehending, she didn't blink.

We wanna get you anyway **cleverclogs!**

I noticed that since I was talking back, kids were gathering round.

said Scott, her second-in-command.

"Go on then," said Toecaps, giving me a warm-up push.

Now, since I was in a bit of a flap and hadn't exactly had any beaming practice, I will admit I thought a little short-term.

I *should* have thought Mars or Jupiter or Australia or the Moon. But I didn't.

What I thought was

Anyway, the next thing I knew,
the next thing any of us knew,
Marigold was no longer
standing in front of me.

She was quietly appearing, bit
by bit, in the playground
plane tree.

Chapter Nine

And The Black Hole Goes Crazy

There was a gigantic gasp. And then an awesome silence as everyone tried to come to terms with what they'd just seen.

"Marigold Barnes!" This was Mr Hines the lunch-break teacher, breaking the silence.

Well, as I now know, beamed objects or people take at least ten minutes to re-settle into themselves. Toecaps couldn't even *hear* what Mr Hines was saying let alone do anything.

All she did was hang there, looking like her knicker elastic wasn't going to hold.

"Who is responsible for this?" Mr Hines yelled. "How did she get up there in the first place?"

Scott stepped up.

By now I was as cool as ice.

"I'll get the caretaker," said Mr Hines, "to bring a ladder."

But as things turned out, he needn't have bothered. A ladder wasn't going to help Toecaps now.

For, as she hung there recomposing herself, the Black Hole began to move towards her.

"NO!" I yelled, "NO!"

But try telling the sun not to shine or the snow not to snow.

It just went on blethering over through the branches like a drunk cloth cape.

And then it went

which no one could hear except Wilf, Eric and me; and Marigold Toecaps Garotter Barnes was no more.

Chapter Ten

Not Nearly The End Of It

Well, I must say, almost immediately the atmosphere in our playground changed completely.

For a start, we all dared breathe again.

But, obviously, that wasn't the end of it. Especially for me, since I couldn't stop thinking about someone *being no more*, all because I hadn't beamed her to Australia.

I was also cross with Wilf for not having his slurpy charge under better control.

So the moment we got home I cleared out one of my cupboards until there was nothing in it but a few specks of dust.

"And here," I said firmly, "is where the Black Hole is to be kept as long as it's in this house."

And another thing. Isn't it time you joined the rest of your lot Wilf? In the atmosphere?

"I'm sure it is," said Wilf, putting the Black Hole into the empty cupboard while I slammed and locked the door.

Ohhh - Do you have to go? I'm just enjoying being clever.

whined Eric.

"Well, if the Slurper's around much longer, you won't be able to enjoy anything," I snapped. "You'll probably be *PLLLTHED* like Toecaps. And so will I."

"Don't take it so hard," said Wilf. "The Black Hole's not as bad as it seems. It doesn't just gobble, you know. It can convert too. Why, by now Toecaps is probably something wonderful, like a field of real marigolds feeding the bees."

I tried to imagine Toecaps being anything wonderful, without much success.

In fact thinking about Toecaps at all only made my guilt worse.

My nerves were getting worse too. I tossed and turned all night while the Black Hole rattled at the cupboard lock. I couldn't stop thinking about the questions that *had* to be asked about Toecap's vanishing.

And when I got to school the next day, they began. Toecap's parents were in the Head's office demanding she find someone to blame immediately.

Then the police descended in force and we all had to go to the hall for questioning.

By this time my guilt and nerves were so bad they seemed to be sizzling through my cheeks in two red patches.

"If any of you," said the senior policeman staring suspiciously at my cheeks, "can think of anything you saw that might help us with our enquiries into the disappearance of Marigold Barnes, I want you to stand up now. Or, if you prefer, come and see me afterwards in Mrs Verge's office."

Well, Eric and I had agreed that we could never mention a visiting Black Hole hanging in a tree, or we'd spend the rest of our lives being called raving bonkers.

So we said nothing.

And since no one else had been *able* to see anything, there was total silence in the hall.

And then, just as I thought I was going to have to blurt everything out, Richard Thomas began to get slowly to his feet.

"Maybe . . . maybe," he stammered.

GOT 'ER?

boomed the police officer.

"Watching, like," Richard stammered bravely on, "it seemed like something from . . . out of space . . . something you couldn't see . . . in the tree . . . just *thlopped* her up . . ."

And once Richard had said it, everyone was saying it. The hall erupted with kids yelling,

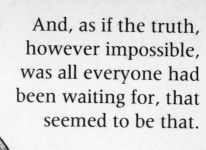

And, as if the truth, however impossible, was all everyone had been waiting for, that seemed to be that.

Toecaps' parents seemed to shrivel like tired, leaky balloons. The police officer coughed and shuffled his papers and announced that he would be following some other lines of enquiry.

Then our Head announced that she and the staff would be opening up the whole Subject Of Bullying in our school but, for the moment, we should all put the matter out of our minds.

Chapter Eleven

And Wilf And The B.H. Leave Us At Last

That, however, was easier said than done for some of us.

When we got home we found the Black Hole had somehow slipped out of the cupboard and *thlopped* my pillows, Eric's pyjamas, his petrol station and all his cars.

He was furious. Though not half as furious as my mother.

WHERE ARE THEY?

When our dad got home she sent him up to give us a serious talking to about the seriousness of hiding things and then lying about it.

It's no good Wilf, you'll have to leave tonight.

Though you can visit us again so long as you don't bring a Black Hole!

"OK," said Wilf, snuggling down in a fold in my duvet as if he had no intention of going anywhere for centuries.

I got out my homework and slapped it on the table in a real sulk. What was it going to take to get the Plllther, Thllopper and Slurper out of my life?

I picked up a pencil and started writing angrily, speaking through clenched teeth as I wrote:

Carbon dioxides and monoxides, ammonias and CFC's. If something isn't done about them soon, kids will have no oxygen to breathe.

To this day I don't know what effect I expected those words to have, if any. But at the word "oxygen" there was an eerie rattle from the cupboard and Wilf leapt from the bed, burning brightly.

"Right, we're off," he said. "Open up."

I had barely unlocked the cupboard when he was swooping on the Black Hole and frog-marching it to the window.

I'll see you soon. Next time we'll have even more fun.

he said, briskly.

And they were gone, flickering away into the night sky.

For a while we stood waving silently. But when we turned back to my room, we had to stuff our mouths with duvet or scream the house down.

Chapter Twelve

The Shock Of The New

Peering out of the Black Hole's cupboard was a face. A face we knew and a face we didn't.

And although we knew it couldn't be, it began to dawn on us that it was. In a new version.

Ttttoecaps?.. I managed.

"Pure Marigold, now," came her tinkly reply. And stepping out, in a bright yellow dress and orange shoes, she twirled round my room as if she'd taken leave of her senses.

But... What... happened?

stammered Eric.

Here, she kissed me on the cheek and, fluttering her paintbrush-eyelashes, continued.

"The only mystery is how I came to be in your cupboard. Still, we won't worry about minor details. I should be getting home as my parents must be worried sick."

A few moments later, as we sat there gobsmacked, our mother came in.

she said, going over to close the cupboard.

As she spoke she was peering into the cupboard. Then further in and further in.

While she was this and this-ing, she was grabbing things from the empty cupboard, like a conjuror from a hat, and throwing them on to the bed.

And there it all was.

my pens

Eric's pyjamas

...and jacket

my trainers

pillows

the cars

the petrol station

and the lunch boxes

And though the lunches were gone, everything else was in one piece, if slightly sucked out of shape as though by a greedy Hoover.

"So it *was* a practical joke!" our mother exploded. "Well, not a very funny one and there will certainly be consequences."

For a start - your games machine is confiscated for a month.

Hardly a crisis, I thought, at that moment.

What was terrifying me now was the fear that it *was* all a practical joke by Wilf and the Black Hole. And, just as our things had turned up unchanged, Toecaps was going to turn up in *her* original version.

But, as it was, I needn't have sweated.

The next day, the completely and utterly converted Marigold was in the playground. Twirling and tinkling around, telling everyone, including the Head, that her transformed character was all due to me.

Soon, the whole school was saying that by the simple act of standing up to her, I'd single-handedly rid the playground of the poisonous Marigold.

Talk about being an overnight hero. I felt about twelve foot high and Eric said he felt ten foot, just for being my brother.

It seemed a lot sweeter than being clever.

And every night since, I stand at my window and think-through to Wilf, wherever he is.